POKéMON
DESTINY DEOXYS

DEOXYS' SECRET

Adapted by Tracey West

SCHOLASTIC INC.

New York   Toronto   London   Auckland   Sydney
Mexico City   New Delhi   Hong Kong   Buenos Aires

ISBN 0-439-74144-0

12 11 10 9 8 7 6 5 4 3 2 1   5 6 7 8 9/0

Printed in the U.S.A.
First printing, March 2005

In the cold, cold North, scientists worked on an ice field.

Suddenly, meteors fell from the sky!

Professor Lund was there with his son, Tory. They watched a strange Pokémon walk across the ice.

The Pokémon, Deoxys, picked up a glowing crystal. Deoxys looked sad.

Then another Pokémon flew down from the sky. Mighty Rayquaza attacked Deoxys.

Rayquaza blasted Deoxys with Hyper Beam. Deoxys broke into pieces. All that was left was a crystal. The crystal sank to the bottom of the icy sea.

The scientists had to escape Rayquaza.
They flew off in a helicopter.
But first, Lund grabbed the crystal that had
fallen from space.

Four years went by. Ash and his friends Max, May, and Brock went to Larousse City. There were machines everywhere.

Robots watched over the city. One robot gave them each a card.

"This is your passport," the robot said. "You will need it to get around town."

Ash met some new Pokémon trainers in Larousse City.

Rafe had Blaziken, a Fire / Fighting Pokémon. He lived in town with his sisters, Audrey and Kathryn. Their friends Sid and Rebecca trained Pokémon, too.

Ash also met Professor Lund and Tory.

After that night on the ice field, Tory was afraid of Pokémon.

"My son will not even touch Pokémon," Lund explained. "He does not have many friends."

"Maybe I can be his friend," Ash said. "He can get to know me and Pikachu. Then he might not be afraid of Pokémon anymore."

"Pika! Pika!" Pikachu agreed.

But Tory was afraid. He went to his father's lab. He liked to sit in the garden there.

If he sat very quietly, bright lights would appear. Tory liked to talk to the lights.

"I am your friend," he called out softly.

Meanwhile, Deoxys had grown back its missing pieces over the years. It broke out of its icy prison in the sea.

Deoxys wanted to find the lost crystal. And Deoxys knew where to look. The Pokémon flew toward Larousse City.

Deoxys let loose with an Aurora Beam, trying to find the crystal. Beautiful lights filled the
sky. Deoxys flew on, searching.

Ash and his friends saw the lights from the park. Tory was with them.

The trainers all released their Pokémon. Tory stood back, afraid to touch them. Tory was almost brave enough to touch Pikachu, but a Cor-phish got in the way.

Even though Tory was still afraid, he trust-
ed his new friends. He brought them all to his
father's lab. He took them to the garden and
showed them the lights.

Up in the sky, Deoxys felt life coming from the crystal. Deoxys knew it was close by. But the signals from the robots and machines were getting in the way.

Deoxys blasted Larousse City with Psycho Boost. The attack messed up all of the robots and machines.

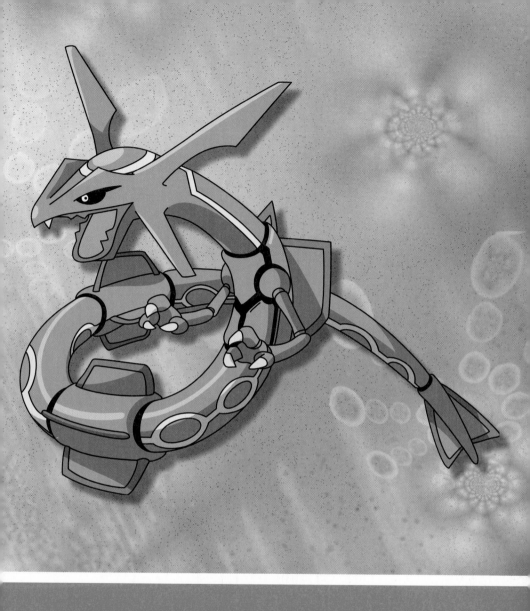

Officer Jenny was watching the skies. She saw another Pokémon coming to town . . . Rayquaza!

Officer Jenny called Lund. "Get everyone out of town," he said. "If Rayquaza and Deoxys battle again, there will be trouble!"

Ash and the others heard the warning. They tried to leave the lab. But the Psycho Boost had shut down all of the computers!

"We can't get out!" Tory cried.

Outside, Rayquaza zoomed toward Deoxys. Deoxys used Aurora Beam. A shield made of light covered the city like a bubble. Rayquaza could not get through!

Ash and his friends pushed through the door. They found Professor Lund's assistant, Yuko, in a secret lab.

Yuko told them the story of Deoxys.

"This crystal fell to Earth the night Deoxys battled Rayquaza," Yuko said. "We think it is another Deoxys."

The crystal began to glow. Sparkling lights came out of it and danced in front of Tory.

"You mean my friend in the garden is a Deoxys?" Tory asked.

Yuko nodded. "Yes. And I think the other Deoxys is looking for it."

"Maybe we can help bring them together," Ash said.

"We have been trying to bring this Deoxys to life," Yuko explained. "We had almost done it when the power went out."

"We could use the wind machine," Rebecca said. "We just need people power to do that."

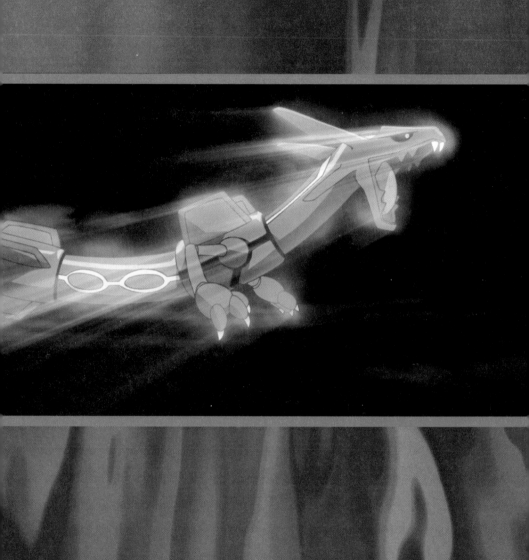

Tory led the way to the wind machine. Above them, Rayquaza broke through the aurora barrier. It headed right for Deoxys.

Ash and Rafe gathered everyone left in town. They told them all to go to the wind machine.

The wind machine had enough power —
almost.

Pikachu helped. So did a cute Plusle and
Minun.

"Let's go," Tory said. "We have to find your friend."

The Deoxys picked up Ash, Tory, and Pikachu. They flew into the sky. They found Rayquaza battling the first Deoxys.

But Rayquaza was not all they had to worry about.

The robots in town went crazy! They joined together to make huge robots. The huge robots attacked Rayquaza. The two Deoxys stood side by side to protect Rayquaza. The robots scooped up Ash, Pikachu, and Tory. They caught Plusle and Minun, too.

Professor Lund had an idea. He told Tory to put his passport into one of the big robots.

The huge robots stopped attacking. They began to fall apart. Ash, Tory, and the three Electric Pokémon fell to the ground.

"Deoxys, save us!" Tory yelled.

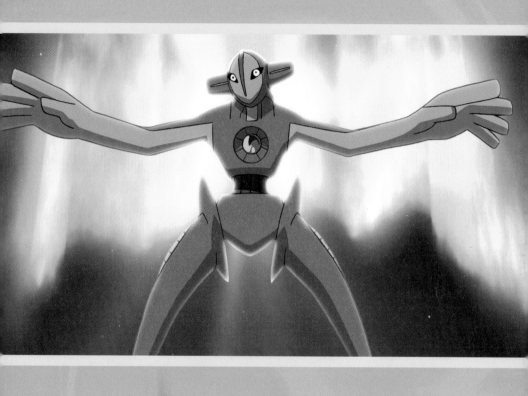

Tory's Deoxys friend caught them just in time. The other Deoxys held Rayquaza in its arms. It used its aurora light to heal Rayquaza. Rayquaza flew off. The battle was over!

It was time for the two Deoxys to leave.

"Good-bye," Tory said. "I will always be your friend."

Everyone was glad to be safe.

Ash hugged Pikachu.

Plusle and Minun hugged Tory. He hugged them back!

"I am not afraid of Pokémon anymore," Tory said.

"Good for you, Tory," Ash said. "This is a happy ending."

In the cold, cold North, the two Deoxys flew across the ice field.

It was a happy ending for them, too!